Just Until Christmas

CAROLE TOWRISS

Four Diamonds
PUBLISHING

COPYRIGHT © 2015 CAROLE TOWRISS
All rights reserved.
ISBN-13: 978-0692705216
Cover photo by Michael Simons
Cover font Monsieur Le Doulaise by Alejandro Paul
and Charles P Bluemlein of Sudtipos
All rights reserved.

No portion of this book (except for excerpts for reviews) may be reproduced in any form without written permission from the publisher.

Scripture quotations are taken from the HOLY BIBLE, NEW INTERNATIONAL VERSION ®. Copyright © 1973, 1978, 1984 by International Bible Society. Used by permission of Zondervan.

All rights reserved.
Any emphasis to scripture quotations is added by the author.

Just Until Christmas is a work of fiction. Names, characters, places, and incidents are either a product of the author's imagination or are used fictitiously. Any resemblance to actual persons, living or dead, events, or locales is entirely coincidental.

To Colleen, Susan, Lynn, and all our children —
Emma, Mira, Dara, and Johnny;
Kendra and Camden;
Ryan and Emily; & Braeden,
Ethan and Miranda
in celebration of all our summer weeks
at "Brandon Beach"

Wait in hope,
Carole

*"We wait in hope for the LORD;
He is our help and our shield.
In Him our hearts rejoice,
for we trust in His holy name.
May Your unfailing love be with us,
LORD, even as we put our hope in You."
~Psalm 33:20-21*

Chapter One

Hope Aristov parked her green Chevy Cruze in front of the weathered blue house on Ocean View Parkway. Slipping the parking pass over her rearview mirror, she climbed out and stared at the cottage that would be her prison for the next three months.

The screened-in porch looked inviting at least—a couple rocking chairs, a wicker couch and love seat, an array of potted plants. Wind chimes tinkled softly in the faint breeze.

She lugged her suitcases onto the porch, then dug through her oversized purse for the keys and opened the front door.

It was nicer than she remembered. The rental agency must have bought some new furniture. Sunlight poured through the tall windows in the front room. A farmhouse table and long benches occupied the back right, and a door led from that into the kitchen to the left. The staircase ran along the left front of the house. Hope threw open all the windows to allow a cross breeze, setting blue-and-white-striped cotton curtains aflutter.

It was only five o'clock, but she was exhausted. She'd packed all morning, argued one last time with her boss—which gave her a later start than she wanted—and then drove the three hours from the Maryland suburbs of DC to the eastern shore.

She yanked off the sheet covering the couch and collapsed on it. She was here. Now what? Hunger gnawed at her stomach. When had she last eaten? Breakfast? She wandered into the kitchen. The refrigerator was empty, all but turned off. Readied for winter. She turned the refrigerator and freezer back to their normal temperatures and rummaged through the pantry. Bare.

Her cell phone rang and she pulled the device from her back pocket. "Yes, Steve." She barely managed to hide the bitterness in her voice.

"Just called to see if you got there all right."

"Don't you have meetings to go to?"

"It's a long drive for one person. I know. I wanted to make sure you were OK."

"Sure."

"I said I was sorry." She could imagine him drawing circles on his yellow legal pad, as he did whenever he didn't really know what to say.

"I think it's pretty clear you planned this from the beginning. Sorry doesn't cut it."

"You'll have another chance in a couple months."

"Whatever. I'm really tired. I'll call in a couple days."

"Hope—"

She punched the end button, harder than necessary. Some partner.

Hadn't she seen a small grocery store on her way in? It would be outrageously expensive this close to the beach, but she was in no mood to drive several miles back out of town to the nearest major chain grocery.

After stepping into the powder room, she splashed water on her face and dried it, then redid her hair up into a high ponytail. She frowned at one more glance in the mirror. Not great, but who was she trying to impress?

She locked the door and headed toward Main Street. The salt smell of the ocean filled the air, relaxing her in spite of herself. An older lady planting flower bulbs in her front yard smiled and waved at her. That never happened back in Bethesda.

Ice machines lined up like sentries outside the store, a one-story building with a brick face. A yellow-striped awning stretched across the front. Hope strode to the refrigerator section and grabbed a half-gallon of milk, a block of Monterey Jack and a dozen eggs. Moving to the right she selected a head of lettuce and one tomato. She looked at a small turkey breast, but groaned at the price and replaced it. Her chef's salad would be meatless tonight.

A red-headed girl smacking gum and wearing large hoop earrings leaned against the counter near the cash register. "Welcome to Surf Foods." She called out the prices in a New Jersey accent so thick she must have moved here last week.

Hope grimaced as she paid—far too much, if you asked her.

Back at the house she found a pan and set water to boil for a couple eggs, and tried not to think about the events that sent her to Brandon Beach, Delaware.

She located the linen closet upstairs, and made up the master bedroom that took up most of the eastern half. Like the rest of the house, the furniture in this room sported a cheerful beach house theme, which did nothing to brighten her mood. Across the hall lay two smaller rooms, each with two twin beds. After opening the windows, Hope trudged back down to eat dinner. Alone.

Chapter Two

"CAN'T YOU EVER BE PATIENT?" From the Surf Foods cash register, Ian MacKay looked over his shoulder at his old college roommate. Standing in the door of the tiny office, Rob nearly reached the top of the doorframe. He had four inches on Ian, but Ian figured he could still take him if he had to. Rob was tall but slender, and Ian was all muscle.

At times like this, he was tempted to take him out. Or at least, send him back to California.

Rob quirked a brow. "We were working, and you just left."

"To wait on a customer! If I don't serve the customers, we won't have any. And without them, we won't have a business to argue about."

Rob laughed. "I didn't realize we were arguing."

Ian narrowed his eyes. "With you it's always arguing."

"Well, why isn't anyone scheduled to be behind the counter at this time of day?"

"Amy's late, as usual." Ian looked toward the door. "Here she comes."

Can we talk about this elsewhere?" He shooed Rob to the back and into the alley, closing the door behind them.

His roommate shrugged. "Dude, if she's such a bad employee, fire her. I don't understand the dilemma."

"She's not that bad." Ian dropped himself onto a stack of wooden crates.

"You complain about her all the time." Rob took the nerf ball from his pocket and bounced it at the wall, catching it on its return.

"There's a lot you don't know." Ian stood to pace. "Look, if we're going to be partners, you have to trust me. You're going to have to assume I know what I'm talking about, and that usually I know more than you about what goes on around here. I grew up here. In Brandon Beach and in this store."

Rob put up his hands in mock surrender. "All right, all right."

Ian faced Rob and folded his arms over his chest. "That said, I will say fresh eyes are a good thing. Now, what ideas do you have that will make it worth my putting up with you?"

"What is this space out here, where we're standing? Why is the alley behind your store wider than everywhere else?"

"Back when this was a bakery, the ovens were here. This wall has steel in it up to about five feet, so we can't tear it down and expand, if that's your thought. Besides, it would only give us about ten more feet. I don't think it would be worth the expense."

"Not for selling space. But you do the books at home, right? Take the money home, count it, balance the books, then take the deposit to the bank?"

"Yeah, so?"

"So how much time do you spend on that each week? What if we built an office—a proper office—in this space? We put in tinted glass, raise the floor to get over the five-foot mark. You do all the paperwork here, and you can keep an eye on things at the same time. You aren't lugging home documents or money, and everything stays locked up here where it belongs. Some of those times you had to schedule two people, now you can have one, because one of us would be here to step in if it got really busy."

Ian halted, ran his hand through his hair. "That's actually a great idea. That alone might make it worth keeping you around."

"My initial investment would more than take care of construction. There would be plenty left over for all my other brilliant ideas."

Ian laughed, then stuck out his hand. "Welcome to Surf Foods."

Later that day, as Rob worked the phone lining up contractor bids, Ian watched the pretty blonde as her ponytail bounced to the back of the store, then juggled her items in her arms on the way back.

The girl—make that young woman—placed her selections on the counter and drew the back of her hand across her brow, looking everywhere but at him. The emerald green t-shirt she wore matched her eyes. He knew all of the year-round residents of the one-mile-square town, but she was new.

"Hot for September, huh?"

"I guess." She still didn't make eye contact.

He rang up her order and quoted the total.

She frowned and pulled two bills from the back pocket of her jeans.

"Everything OK?"

"Your prices are ridiculous."

He shrugged. "Land and taxes are expensive out here. Gotta make a living."

"Yeah." She picked up her bags and stalked out.

Ian smiled and shook his head. Beautiful girl. Lousy attitude.

Chapter Three

HOPE PULLED HER LAPTOP FROM its foam-lined contoured bag and placed it on the dining room table, followed by several comb-bound stacks of paper. She plugged in the computer and pushed the power button. Now where had she jotted down the wifi password? She reached for her smartphone and scanned through the emails until she found the one she'd sent to herself, then entered the code and connected to the internet.

Her email showed nothing of interest. Why should it? Who would care that she left?

She pulled the first manuscript toward her. *Software Configuration Management Systems for Postsecondary Educational Institutions.* Sighing, she turned the cover page, to the instructions on the next page. "Rewrite for non-technical decision makers at graduate levels." She placed her fingers on the keys.

Four hours later, she turned the last page, hit save once again and stood. She massaged her neck, trying to work out the kinks. If she intended to stay here for three months, she'd definitely need a better chair.

She filled her water bottle from the sink and stepped onto the porch. The warm, late September breeze and the sound of crashing waves beckoned from the beach only two blocks east. One good thing about the cottage, anyway.

She crossed the empty parking lot at the end of the road and stepped onto the worn wood walkway that crossed over the dune grass to the white sand. As the structure reached its highest point, she halted and pulled in a deep breath. She'd always loved that smell.

The deserted beach stretched for miles on either side of her. Sandpipers skittered in and out of the waves, bobbing their long bills in the sand in search of food. Seagulls wandered aimlessly, the summer guests with french fries and bread long gone.

Hope kicked off her flip-flops and left them at the end of the walkway. She strolled to the water's edge and waded in. Tiny shells thrown onto the sand at her feet rolled back into the water, then were tossed out again. Watching the waves roll in, one after another, never-ending, perfectly consistent, somehow felt reassuring. Even the noise soothed her.

She backed up a few feet and sat, digging her toes into the warm sand. The sun shone on her shoulders, and seagulls called overhead.

If she hadn't been forced to come here, she might have truly enjoyed it. A few days, even a week or two might prove to be quite relaxing.

But knowing she was stuck here until late December sucked all the joy from it.

She had to admit it had come at a good time. After what Steve had done to her, there was no way she could have worked alongside him in the office and remained calm. At least Teresa consented to her working from here, so she could keep her job.

But she shouldn't have to. Just because Steve *stole* that promotion out from under her. Lying, cheating Steve.

And Teresa let him get away with it. It wasn't fair.

Chapter Four

AT NINE AM ON THE last Monday of September, Ian, his father, and Rob sat at a large, round table in the conference room of Cooper, Koenig & Barton. Ice, glasses and water sat on a tray in the center.

Stanley Barton, a rotund, balding man who wore too much aftershave, sat across from the trio with a stack of papers. He adjusted his glasses and reordered the papers for the fifth time.

An assistant who couldn't be more than twenty years old brought in a tray of colas and sandwich cookies and placed it in the middle of the table.

"Thank you, darling. Now we can begin." His thick southern accent had always seemed out of place in Delaware.

"You're welcome, Uncle Stan." She pranced out of the room, dark hair flipping side to side.

"Susie's a sophomore this year. Her dad's hoping she'll go to law school when she graduates, continue the family tradition. She helps out around here when she's not in class."

"Well, she's lovely," said Dad. "I'm sure she'll do fine."

Stan looked over his shoulder at the closed door before he spoke. "Thank you, Sean, but truth be told, she's not the brightest crayon in the box. I don't think it will happen."

Ian choked on his Coke. "Stan!"

The older man peered at him over his glasses. "What do you want me to do? Lie?"

"Well, no ..."

Rob laughed. "An honest lawyer. Imagine that."

Stan fixed him with a glare and Rob stopped short, a blush creeping up his neck.

Stan cleared his throat. "You're one of them L.A. boys, aren't you?"

"Yes, sir."

Stan stared a few moments more and then burst into laughter. "We'll get along just fine, then, son. Welcome to Brandon Beach."

Rob let out a long breath and chuckled.

Stan picked up the first stack. "Now, Sean, you're selling Surf Foods to Ian and Rob? Isn't this rather sudden?"

"Well, yes and no. I'd always planned to hand it over, of course, in time. But Marie's condition is worsening far quicker than anyone realized it would. She doesn't trust anyone but me, and I want to be there for her. Ian has his MBA, as does Rob. He can run the store better than I can. But I don't have enough saved up yet to retire; I was planning on working another ten years or so." He cleared his throat. "Then Ian mentioned the possibility of an investor. Rob's moved here and is going to invest enough to update the store some as well as allow me to retire and care for Marie."

Ian's heart clenched as he listened to his dad. His mother had always been the strong one, the delight of his life. Seeing her fall deeper and deeper into Alzheimer's nearly ripped him in two every time he came home. How could his father handle it so calmly and practically, watching

Just Until Christmas

his wife of forty years literally lose her mind? It had to be only by the grace of God.

Rob's hand on his back jerked him back to the proceedings. Papers were being shoved in front of him. Rob pointed to lines on the bottom of the page with colorful sticky arrows that ordered him to "sign here." He affixed his signature to more pages than he thought could possibly be necessary, then slumped back in his chair as Rob handed over a check to Stan.

"This will go into escrow until all the necessary papers have been filed, taxes and fees paid, et cetera, et cetera. Should all be finalized by the end of the week." He stood and held out his hand. "Congratulations, gentlemen. You are now property owners in the great town of Brandon Beach."

Ian and Rob shook Stan's hand, and Rob tried to shake Dad's, but he was drawn into a bear hug instead.

"Take care of my boy for me, Rob."

"I'll do my best, sir."

Ian followed Rob out of the room, but returned when he realized he forgot his suit coat.

Stan had his arm around Dad. "Give my best to my cousin, will you?"

"I'll do that, Stan." He stepped away, then turned back. "Will you mail your bill?"

"No charge, Sean."

"Stan, don't be ridiculous—"

"Sean, it was an easy transaction. Took no time at all. Consider it my gift to Marie."

Dad dropped his gaze to the floor and was silent a moment. "Thanks, Stan." His voice cracked.

Ian hustled back to Rob, not wanting his father to know he'd seen the exchange. But when Dad caught up with them, Ian could not miss the tear in his eye.

Ian reached up and slid the bolt on the door up into the doorframe, then reached down and pushed the other one into the floor. He pulled the second door closed behind him and threw the dead bolt. He was just about to turn around when a familiar blond ponytail rushed up.

"Please!" Green eyes pleaded from under blond side swept bangs. She held her hands in front of her in mock prayer.

He flipped the dead bolt back and opened the door just an inch. "What do you need?"

"Please. I've been working hard all week. I really, really need some ice cream. I'm begging you."

Ian couldn't resist. "Even at these ridiculous prices?"

She grimaced. "I'm so sorry. That was rude. You're right. I'll come back tomorrow." She turned away.

"No, no, no. Come back." He waved her in.

"I don't want to get you in trouble."

"It's OK. It's my father's store." Technically, still his father's. At least until the papers were filed at the courthouse. It was almost his, but he didn't want her to know that. Yet.

"You're sure?"

He chuckled. "Come on. Get your ice cream."

Her smile lit up her face and warmed his heart. He followed her to the back.

She grabbed some french vanilla, a container of chocolate syrup and a gallon of milk.

"Milk?"

She blushed. "Milkshake."

He laughed. "You just move in?"

"Mm-hmm."

"Where?"

"Over on Ocean View."

He took the gallon jug from her and walked her to the cash register.

"Which block?"

"200s."

The only possible place she could have moved into was the one managed by Jensen's. No one else had sold. "The rental place?"

"You ask a lot of questions."

"Sorry. Just trying to be friendly."

"Yes. It belonged to my father."

He placed the items in a paper bag and told her the total.

As she handed him the money, she asked, "Do you know of a reputable plumber? I need a few things repaired."

"Major things? Or little things?"

Just the slightest smile appeared. "Really? More questions?"

He laughed. "I just mean I can fix a lot of things. I do a lot around the store to save us money, and I'd be happy to help, if you want. Plumbers can be expensive."

She eyed him for a moment or two. "I barely know you."

"We can do it in the middle of the day, leave the windows open, keep your cell phone in your pocket with 911 on speed dial. I can even give you references."

She chuckled. "OK. I could really use the savings. When's good for you?"

"I'm off tomorrow. You?"

She wrinkled her nose. "I'm off every day."

"Drop by around 2?"

"I'll be there."

Chapter Five

THE RED-HEAD WAS WORKING at Surf Foods. Hope grabbed a dozen eggs—the one thing she'd forgotten at the chain store this morning. She placed the eggs on the counter, and this time instead of popping her gum, the girl glared at Hope.

On the way home, Hope tried to recall if she had done anything to offend the girl. She couldn't think of a thing.

That afternoon, Hope leaned against the doorframe and admired the tanned, muscular legs clad in jeans shorts sticking out from under her sink. One leg bent at the knee, the other remained straight. His feet ended in new running shoes.

After a few moments of clanks, clunks and an occasional grunt, Ian set a rusted garbage disposal on the floor, and felt around unsuccessfully for the new one. Twisting, he stuck his head out from the cabinet.

Hope arched her brows. "Having trouble?"

Ian grinned. "Why don't you make yourself useful and hand me the screwdriver in a minute."

She stepped closer and knelt next to him.

His head disappeared again as he took the disposal with him. After a moment he stuck out a hand.

She placed the tool in his palm.

He closed his fingers over the screwdriver and her fingers. His touch sent warmth up her arm, and she jerked it away.

He attached the unit, jiggled it, and then scooted out of the small space, sitting before her with his arms on his knees. His tousled light brown hair fell just over the collar of his yellow polo shirt, and the day's worth of stubble set off his strong jaw.

"I fixed the dripping faucet and running toilet—"

"Already?"

"They were easy. Just a washer for the faucet and an adjustment for the toilet. So now I'll flip the breaker switch and check this, and we're all set."

Wow. How much money had he saved her? "How can I possibly thank you?"

"I'll give you the receipt." He winked.

"But what about your time? Wh- what can I do to compensate you? Surely you have better things to do."

"How about a walk? Or maybe one of those milkshakes you are obviously very practiced at making?"

"Obviously?" She put her hands other hips and glanced down her body. Was he implying she was fat?

"Whoa, whoa! I was just referring to your little setup there." He gestured to the counter, where she had a blender, a tall glass with a long spoon set in it, and a large bottle of chocolate syrup sitting on a place mat.

"Oh ..." She could feel the blush on her cheeks. "A walk?"

"Sure. Or a run? Do you ... ? I noticed your running shoes by the door."

She pointed to his feet. "I see you have a new pair."

Ian tipped one foot on its heel and studied it. "Yeah. Breaking them in. I run most mornings on the beach. I'd love for you to join me." He pinned her with a gentle stare for so long she had to look away.

She stood and turned away. "How about that milkshake first? Then we'll see."

"I'll get the breaker switch." Ian headed to the back of the house, and Hope retrieved the milk and ice cream from the freezer. By the time he'd tested the disposal, she had two tall, chocolate shakes ready.

Ian pulled out two kitchen chairs. "So, what brought you out here?"

"Long story. I'm here from Bethesda."

"Why's that?"

She shifted in her seat. "I forgot how quiet it gets after Labor Day."

Ian gave her a quizzical look, but didn't pursue his question. "Yeah. Summer's a double-edged sword. Busy and noisy, but store owners like us have to make almost all our money in those three to four months, so the more tourists the better. I'm in a little better position since I sell groceries, and not souvenirs, but still..." He took a long slurp of his shake.

"Wait—'store owners like us'? *You* own the store? You said it was your dad's."

"The store *was* my dad's that day, but he's retired now. Now my old college roommate and I own it. " He finished his shake and pushed his glass away. "So what do you miss most about Bethesda?"

"Well ... it sounds silly."

"Try me."

She emptied her glass as she considered whether or not she should trust him. His warm blue eyes convinced her to chance it. "I actually missed it in Bethesda, too."

"I don't understand."

"I had a cat. She died about three months ago. She got sick and I had to put her to sleep. She was a tortie—"

His brows furrowed. "A what?"

"A tortie. Tortoise shell-colored. She'd sit in my lap sometimes at night—if she wanted to, she was kind of moody—when I read." Hope stared out the window. "And I had this spray that was a kind of a shampoo, waterless, that made her smell like a blueberry muffin." She smiled. "I loved that smell. She'd get so mad when I sprayed her, but then I'd brush it all over her, and she loved that part." She pulled her gaze back to Ian to find him staring at her.

"Sorry. I didn't mean to go on and on."

"What was her name?"

"Frisky." She shrugged. "I got her at the shelter and she was already named. But most of the time I just called her Kitty." She tilted her head. "You're not going to laugh at me?"

"Why would I?"

"I don't know. Most guys usually do when I talk about her. Even when she was alive they did." She shrugged.

He chuckled. "Maybe you hung out around the wrong guys." He stood and walked his glass to the sink, then turned around and leaned against it. "I have a lot of paperwork to do, so I've got to shove off. But will you go running with me tomorrow?"

She hesitated.

"Please? I get lonely out there." A wide smile brought out dimples on either side his mouth.

"I am quite sure that is a huge lie." She laughed.

"Main Street boardwalk. 7:30. Will you come?"

"No promises." No way was she getting involved with anyone here. Not even someone as nice and good-looking as Ian.

Chapter Six

IAN GLANCED AT THE CLOCK as he rang up a customer. 9:25. Amy was late again. He was compassionate, but this was getting to be a real problem. Maybe Rob was right, he needed to fire—the front door opened and Amy sauntered in, smacking her gum.

"Amy, we need to talk."

"Yeah?"

"You've got to make more of an effort to get here on time for your shifts."

She eyed him as she tied on her yellow apron. "I haven't been late all that often."

"You've been late more often than not. Would you like to see my notes?"

"Does this have to do with her?"

"Her?"

"The blonde."

"Hope? Of course not. Why would it? This has to do with my being able to count on you being here when you're supposed to be. I realize you have complications, but I need you to be here when you're scheduled. Can you do that?"

"Yeah." She played with her hair.

Was she even paying attention? "If you can't, I'll have to find someone who can."

"Like her?"

"No, not her. I have to go. Rob will be here in a couple hours, before the lunch rush."

"Whatever." Amy crossed her arms and spun away from him.

Ian headed north to Ocean View Parkway, then turned left to Hope's house. He took all three porch steps at once, pushed open the screen door and then rapped on the inner door.

Hope appeared at the door in a cherry red tank top and white shorts that showed off her long legs. His smile made her blush. "Ummm…hi?"

"Let's go swimming."

"Now?"

"It's 85 degrees out. It's probably one of the last nice days we'll have this year."

She grimaced.

"Come on, please? You owe me."

She scoffed. "I owe you? How's that?

"You haven't shown up for a run yet. It's been two weeks."

"I said no promises, but *fine*, I'll swim with you." She laughed. "Let me get my suit on. You may as well come in." She headed upstairs and he sat on the edge of the couch. Books were on the end table; stacks of DVDs sat next to the TV. A blanket and pillow were tossed on the chair—had she been sleeping on the couch?

She bounced down the stairs in flip-flops and a white terry cover-up, a red and blue striped towel in hand. "OK. Let's go." She flashed him an uneasy smile, and guilt set in.

"We don't have to. I shouldn't have pushed. Want to do something else?" He cringed. "Or…or I can just go."

"No, it's fine. The waves looked a little rough the other day, that's all. I was never big on swimming in the ocean. I'm more of a sit-and-read-on-the-beach girl."

"Seriously, let's do something else, then. We can hit the outlet malls in Rehoboth Beach, go shopping."

"Oh, no, we're going." Pointing at him, she laughed. "But if I drown, it's your fault. *And* you owe me shopping some other day."

Any time. "All right. I won't let you drown, I promise." He opened her front door, and followed her out, grabbing the towel he'd tossed on the wicker chair on his way in.

Ten minutes later they stood on the sand. "Come on, it's better to do it all at once."

"Just a minute." She unbelted the cover up, revealing a purple one piece. She sucked in a long breath and winced. "OK."

He grabbed her hand and ran into the surf. The water was warm and he ducked under an approaching wave. He came up to find her gasping. His chest constricted. Had he pushed her too far? He grasped her shoulders. "Are you OK?"

Her green eyes widened and she stared at him, hand over her mouth, for several seconds.

Oh, God, what have I done? Please let her breathe. His heart raced faster. She'd never speak to him again.

Without warning she burst into laughter.

"Oh, that was fun! Terrifying, but fun!"

Relief washed over him. "Oh, I thought I'd really hurt you!" He closed his eyes and exhaled a forceful breath.

She laughed again. "So did I for a minute."

"Up for more, or done now?"

She answered him by diving farther into the next wave.

They swam for a couple hours, until Ian's stomach begin to rumble. "Are you hungry?"

"Yeah. This works up an appetite."

"Had any beach fries since you've been back?"

"Nope. They still open?"

"Some of them."

After toweling off, he pulled on a T-shirt while she donned her cover up. They crossed the sand and climbed the steps. Boarded-up souvenir shops lined the street side of the boardwalk. At Main Street the walkway opened onto the brick-paved town center, surrounded by boutiques and restaurants. A bandstand sat on the southwest corner, with shiny white benches facing the stage.

About halfway through the center, he grabbed her hand. "Trust me?"

She grinned. "Not sure yet."

He walked though the town center to a place called AB's Fries and at the window, he ordered two fish combos and two large Cokes.

"How do you know I like Coke?"

He pulled out his wallet. "One, I saw an empty can on the coffee table before we left, and two, you get your own drink."

She laughed while he accepted his change.

He grabbed the two cups, handed her one and gestured to the fountain drink machine. "See? What do you want?"

"Coke. What else is there?"

A young worker handed them baskets of deep-fried fish fillets and fries. Ian reached for a yellow metal spice container and sprinkled it liberally over the fries.

She gave him a sideways glance and then followed him back to the benches. The breaded fish was hot, tender and delicious. "Mmm, this is great." She pointed to his fries. "You put Old Bay on your fries?"

"I put Old Bay on everything. Try it."

She stuffed a couple in her mouth. "They're good. A little spicy, but lots of flavor."

"Obviously you're not a native. It's quite popular around here. Pretty regional, though. Got about a dozen different spices in it. My mom puts it in everything. Used to, anyway." His heart ached at the thought of never tasting her cooking anymore.

Chapter Seven

HOPE NOTICED THE FLASH OF ... something ... that crossed his face as he went silent a moment. "What happened to her?"

He winced. "She has Alzheimer's. That's why my dad retired, to take full-time care of her." The pain in his eyes tugged at her heart. What happened to the strong, happy-go-lucky guy she'd come to know?

"I'm sorry. That must be really hard. For all of you." She squeezed his hand.

"Thank you."

"What do you miss the most?"

He blinked. "What?"

"What do you miss the most about her?"

He breathed deeply, put his food down and sat back against the bench resting his elbows along the back. "I miss talking to her. I could tell her everything. She had this way of listening to you that made everything else fade away, you know?"

Just Until Christmas

She did know. He must have gotten it from her.

"She really paid attention. And she never offered cheap platitudes. She often pointed me to the Bible, but she never rushed me through the pain. Sometimes I didn't like that at the time, but in the end, it was good. I ended up growing stronger."

He stared out at the ocean. "She loved the beach. She was the one who was from here, generations back. Dad met her in college, and when they married they moved here. She refused to live anywhere else—said it was a deal-breaker." He smiled, for only a moment. "You know the hardest part?"

Hope shook her head.

"Feeling so helpless. She looks so ... normal. She looks like she's always looked. But she's ... just not."

"What's your favorite memory of her?"

"Wow, that's a tough one. There are so many." He ran his hands through his hair. "She loved Christmas. She loved Christmas decorations, especially lights. She put up so many you'd think we had a decorations store. And they went up Thanksgiving Day. There were lights everywhere, but only on the inside. I asked her once why she didn't decorate the outside. She said it was because she rarely saw the outside—only coming and going—so why waste the time and effort to decorate it? She would sit up at night after everyone went to bed and watch the tree twinkle."

"That sounds beautiful."

"One year, I was sitting with her—I thought it was terribly late but it was probably before nine o'clock because I was around eight years old, and suddenly the entire house went dark. Pitch black. She had blown a fuse!" Ian laughed so hard he could barely talk. "She had bought a whole bunch of extra light strings on sale at the dollar store and put them all up and blew a fuse. We couldn't get it fixed until the next day, so we all piled into mom and dad's room that night and had a slumber party."

Hope chuckled along with him. If only she had such delightful memories. She shoved down her jealousy in order to concentrate on Ian. "That's a wonderful memory. Maybe you should write them down. When things get discouraging, you could look at the book."

He tilted his head. "Sounds like something you would say."

She frowned. "What does that mean?"

"I saw all your books scattered around. You love to read. Probably like to write, too. What do you do, anyway?"

"I'm an editor."

"Ha! I knew it." He slapped his thigh. "What kind of editor?"

"I take work by engineers and scientists, and edit it. I take out all the science-speak, and fix all the grammar and punctuation." She shrugged. "It's not bad. Sometimes I even enjoy it."

"So you're not a writer?"

She shook her head.

"Well, I was close. It's good you can do that from here."

"Yeah, especially now."

"Why now?"

She drew in a long breath. "I just finished a long project for a university with a partner. They loved our work. Trouble is, my partner purposely told me the wrong date for the presentation to them, and went by himself. They raved about him to Teresa—our boss—and he got a promotion. I got nothing."

"I'm sorry. That's really underhanded."

"So it's a good thing I don't have to be there and see him for a while."

"I can understand that." He stared at her until she looked away. "Hey, want some ice cream?" He pointed to the ice cream shop across the way.

"I don't like soft serve."

"They have milkshakes." He said it in a singsong voice.

"I like my own."

"How can you drink so many milkshakes, and not be … um … oh, dear …" Color crept into his cheeks.

Hope laughed. "As big as a house?"
He nodded.
"I run most nights."
"You'll run at night but not with me in the morning." He pouted.
She shrugged. "I like sunsets."
"I'll get you out in the morning yet." He blew out a long breath. "Hey, thanks for asking about my mom. Most people don't know what to say, so they don't say anything."

"My mom died when I was twelve. No one wanted to even mention her name. I know they meant well. I think they thought it would make me too sad. But I wanted to remember her, remember the good things. And it was just me and my dad then, so I had no one to talk to." She winced as the isolation washed over her.

Ian grabbed her hand. "Let's make a deal. Whenever you want to talk about your mom, or I want to talk about mine, we'll be there for each other. OK?"

Did she really trust him enough for that yet? She might not talk about hers, but she'd listen to him any time. "Deal."

Chapter Eight

IAN FOUND HIMSELF COMING UP with excuses to see Hope. If he had the nerve, he'd show up on the beach at sunset to run with her, but that would be a little too obvious. He had promised to take her shopping, though ...

He tugged his cell phone from his back pocket. One ring. Three ... four ... the voice mail kicked in. What should he say? "Ummm ... Hope, this is Ian. I promised I'd take you shopping, so if you're still interested, call me back." He pocketed the phone.

"Who was that?" Rob sauntered up behind him, a fresh cash drawer in hand.

"A girl."

"The blonde." He wiggled his brows.

"Maybe."

Rob laughed. "You're a terrible liar. Aren't you supposed to be gone by now?"

"Yeah, but …"

"Amy's late."

Ian sighed. "Yeah."

"I know you feel bad for her, but we have to do something."

"I know. But what you don't know is, she is a huge support to her family. Her mother is alone, with three other kids besides Amy. Without this job, she'd have to drop out of college. And she can only afford community college at that. If she's late, it's because one of the others was sick or something."

Ian straightened the display of potato chips at the end of the aisle. "She may be annoying as all get-out, but she knows what she's doing, and she's honest. Finding and training someone else would be a huge hassle."

"Then you have to have a talk with her." Rob moved to the register and switched out the drawers. Punching buttons, he started the report tape.

"I already did. Two weeks ago. Apparently didn't do any good. She just kept asking me if it had anything to do with 'the blonde.'"

Rob shook his head. "She has a crush on you, dude."

"She's nineteen!"

"Nineteen-year-olds don't get crushes? That's the perfect age. And she's seriously jealous of Hope."

"There's nothing to be jealous of."

"Sure there's not."

"Not yet anyway."

"Enough for a nineteen-year-old."

Ian shrugged. "I can't help that."

"Maybe I should talk to her, then." He took the used drawer and tape back to the office to lock it up.

"Go ahead." His phone chimed. "Hello."

"Ian?"

He smiled and leaned against the counter. "Hi."

"You called about shopping?"

"Yeah. You still want to go?"

"You don't have to do that. I can't imagine that would be very much fun for a guy."

"No problem. I'd enjoy it. We can go to the outlet malls, maybe get some dinner."

"What if we get lunch first, then go shopping? I'm kind of hungry."

"Sure. Whatever you want. When should I pick you up?"

"Whenever's good for you. I'm open all day."

"Great. I'll be there in thirty minutes." He pushed the end button and slipped it back in his pocket. He looked up to see Rob smirking at him.

"Dude, if you could see your face."

"What?"

"That smile. I've never seen it so wide. Not even with Katie."

"Yeah, well, she just blew me off for dinner. Suggested lunch instead, so, like I said. Nothing to be jealous of."

Rob smirked. "Smile's gone."

"Shut up. I gotta go. You wait for Amy." He tossed his apron at Rob.

"She's not expecting you for thirty minutes. Why the rush?"

"I might be stuck with you in the store now, but I can still kick you out of my apartment." He left to the sound of Rob's laughter.

After going home to wash up and change his shirt three times, Ian arrived at Hope's. Her door was open.

She glanced at her watch. "Are you always so punctual?"

"What?"

"You said thirty minutes exactly twenty-eight minutes ago."

"Sorry. Perils of owning a store, I guess. Gotta open on time."

"Well, it's annoying." She chuckled.

"Fine. Next time I'll be late."

"Next time, huh?"

He grinned. "What are you wanting to shop for? There are three outlet malls in Rehoboth." He gave her a brochure.

"Aren't you prepared." She quirked a brow at him.

He shrugged. "We have a display in the store."

"I need some new cushions for these couches, and the ones out on the porch. I have measurements." She waved a paper at him. "So it's good you'll be there—I'll need some muscle." She squeezed his upper arm.

He sucked in a breath, and she caught his gaze for a moment, then quickly pulled her hand away.

She folded the paper in half, and in half again, then shoved it in her purse. "Well, ummm, we should go."

"Any place in particular you want to eat?"

"I made a half sandwich, so we can wait for dinner if you like." She gave him a smile that nearly stopped his heart.

He needed to be careful not to read anything into that.

"Anything you want." He turned to the door and held it open for her. A whiff of citrus swirled around him as she passed. He closed the door and waited for her to lock it, enjoying her perfume.

After visiting several stores to find just what she needed, including some outside the mall, his stomach was rumbling. He'd skipped lunch after her comment about dinner, but he didn't want to tell her that. He placed the last bag in the back of his Jeep. "So, where would you like to eat?"

"You like Mexican?"

"I love Mexican."

"And you know exactly where there's a great one."

"Not in Rehoboth."

"How about the one we passed when you missed the turn and we had to make a U-turn?" She pointed up the street.

"Funny. Keep it up and you'll go home hungry."

Her face blanched. "I'm sorry. I didn't mean it…"

"Hey, I'm kidding. Don't worry." Wow. She was really skittish. He reached for her arm. "It's fine, really."

She seemed to relax, so he walked her around to her side of the car.

During the meal and on the ride home, she seemed to become more comfortable around him. Most of her life she still kept a carefully guarded fortress though, one he desperately wanted to breach. But he'd happily wait until she was ready.

When they reached her house, he carried her packages to the porch.

"You can just leave them there on the chair." She unlocked the door, then leaned against the frame. "Thanks for everything. I had a really great time."

"So did I. Thanks for coming." He stuffed his hands in his pockets.

"Are you sure you're not mad?"

"About what?" He thought back though the day. "The U-turn comment?"

She nodded.

"Of course not. Although …"

"What?"

"I think now you owe me."

"Owe you what?" She giggled. Good, she'd learned to take his jokes.

"You owe me a run. In the morning."

"Wow. You play dirty."

"I hardly think so. It's been weeks since I asked you."

She grinned. "All right. You win. Tomorrow. Sun up."

"I'll be waiting. He resisted the urge to place his hand on her cheek. "Go on in and lock up."

She smiled and walked in backwards, then closed the door.

Ian climbed in his Jeep and laid his head against the seat.

Had he made a crack in the wall?

Chapter Nine

HOPE LEANED AGAINST THE DOOR. When had she had as much fun as she had today? She couldn't remember. Ian was sweet, funny, charming and impossibly good-looking.

Sooner or later, it would have to come crashing down.

The bad would come out—the need for control, the deceit, the manipulation everybody seemed to be so good at. At least everyone she'd met so far. Chris was perfect when they started dating. Even for the first couple months. Then he had to start going out with every woman in the office behind her back. If he didn't want to be tied down, why didn't he just break up with her? Did he have to lie?

And Steven. Taking credit for all her work just so he could get the promotion. Lying to her about the presentation. Even Teresa letting him get away with it so she could get her own promotion, using Steve as the perfect employee for her reference.

And let's not forget about Marcos…

She was not going to let that happen again. No one would use her, lie to her. She'd keep her guard up. Stick to her plans.

The clock on the wall reminded her the mail would be in by now. She'd have to walk down to the post office and pick it up from her box there. Apparently no mailboxes were allowed in Brandon Beach. Whatever.

She bounded up the stairs, jumped in the shower, changed her clothes and jogged to New York Street. The after-work crowd was easing, but she still had to wait a few moments to get to hers. She unlocked her box, grabbed the stack of letters and circulars and dropped them into the tote slung over her shoulder.

The evening air was warm, with just a slight breeze, so she ambled up Main Street. Most of the shops on the boardwalk were closed, but most of those on Main stayed open all year. A souvenir shop boasted a season-end sale, though that sign had been up since she arrived. She stopped in to browse and discovered beach towels on clearance. The bath towels she'd brought from Bethesda were threadbare. Some extra-long, fluffy towels would be nice. After sorting through what was left—most of which were kind of ugly—she found three that were basic stripes and purchased them.

Back at the intersection of New York and Main, she kissed her fingertips and touched the ragged metal hem of the sailor's coat for luck before she turned left. Old habits, even ones you wanted to forget—buried so deeply you could never find them again—died hard. The bronze statue of the mariner, fists on the ship's wheel and a pipe in his mouth, had stood at this end of town for nearly forty years. Twenty feet tall, it was a landmark for locals and visitors alike. How many times had she met a high school date there?

At home she kicked off her shoes on the porch and put her new towels and swim suit in the wash. She dropped to the couch to sort the mail she'd picked up at the post office. Junk mail, junk mail, junk mail … a letter from Earnst, Peebles & Devons, Attorneys at Law, Chicago,

Just Until Christmas

Illinois.

She ran her fingers over the gold embossed return address, the textured paper of the envelope. They would spend a ridiculous amount on stationery, but would they give someone like her a break? Squeezing her eyes shut a moment first, she ripped open the letter, skimmed through it, and released a long sigh. They'd given her only one more month. Not the three she'd asked for, even after she had explained the situation. She glanced at the signature. Charles Allen Hartford. Another in a long line of people who never stayed in that office long enough to learn her name or care about her situation.

$12,000. Where was she supposed to come up with twelve thousand dollars in one month? If they'd only waited until she could fix up the house and sell it. She'd explained all that in her letter. This wasn't even her fault. She was just cleaning up after *him*.

Again.

Maybe she could use the house to get a short-term loan. The bank here would understand the value of the property and might trust her with the financing.

Fat chance?

She had no job here, no references. Only debt.

The hole just kept getting deeper.

Chapter Ten

IAN PACED THE BOARDWALK AT 7:30. Yes, he was early. He'd tried hard not to be. He couldn't help it. And she'd said no promises. Why was he so attracted to her when he didn't really even know her?

He'd give her ten more minutes.

At 7:35, Hope ran up Main Street.

He stepped to the edge of the walk to meet her. "Didn't get lost, did you?" He could feel the grin on his face. The smile on hers was his reward.

"I haven't been gone that long. Even if I'd never been here I couldn't get lost."

"Hey, don't be making fun of my town, now. Small isn't always bad."

"I suppose not."

"Sand or street?"

"You run on the sand?" Her eyes grew wide as she gazed at the surf.

"Sure. Ever tried it?"

She shook her head, her eyes still fixed on the waves.

Just Until Christmas

Now she had him worried. Maybe this was a bad idea. "Are you OK?"

She set her jaw. "Let's do it."

They hurried down the wood steps and toward the water.

"All right, lean forward, and keep your knees high. It will be a little slower going, but other than that, it's pretty much the same."

They jogged north in the tawny sand for about twenty minutes, then turned back. The beach was almost deserted this time of day. She was obviously a runner, and her stride seemed effortless, even on sand. Her hair, caught up in a ponytail, flew behind her, bouncing rhythmically against her teal t-shirt. He usually preferred running alone, but for some reason he loved running next to her.

Back across from Main Street, he slowed, and was surprised when she glanced over her shoulder and grinned, then sped up. He took the hint, and chased her. The thought of grabbing her around her slender waist and tackling her to the ground crossed his mind, but instead, he passed her, turned and ran backwards, gloating.

"Fine, fine, you win." She held her hands up and laughed, slowing to a walk.

"You asked for it." He chuckled as he returned to her side.

"Yes, I did."

"Don't be surprised if your ankles are sore tomorrow, or your calves. Or both."

Hope laughed. "Oh, now you tell me."

"I could come and massage them if they hurt too much."

"I doubt that will be necessary."

"You may get used to running on sand. Have to do it every day. Or at least a few times a week." He raised a brow.

"I don't think that will happen."

He scanned the horizon. "The beach in the morning is my favorite place in all the world. I think God did his best work on the beach."

Hope huffed.

He shifted his gaze to her. "What?"

She shrugged. "I don't know."

"Don't believe in God?"

"Sure I do. I'm just a little angry with Him at the moment."

"That's OK."

"It is?" She halted and stared at him.

"Sure. He's a big God. He can handle it." He tilted his head. "Would you like to go to church with me on Sunday?"

"I don't think that would be a good idea." She walked away, waving a hand.

"Why not?"

"It's just not." She glanced over her shoulder. "It's been close to an hour. I think I should get back."

She was obviously trying to get away. "Can we run again?"

"Sure. I'll see you at the store. By the way, the last couple times I've been in the store, you know that girl, the one with the red hair?"

"Amy?"

"If you're not there she seems to be very upset with me. She wasn't like that the first time she waited on me, and she's not like that with other customers. But when she rings me up, she just glares at me. I mean, if looks could kill, I'd drop dead right there."

Ian shook his head and chuckled.

"What? Why are you laughing?"

"Rob was right."

"About what?

"He's said for weeks Amy has a crush on me. I think she's jealous of you. When was the first time this happened?"

"Umm ... the morning before you came to fix the plumbing."

"I'd mentioned to Rob I was going to your house. She heard me."

"Well, thanks for getting me on someone's hit list!" She punched his shoulder, and her eyes grew wide. She placed her hand over her mouth.

Ian laughed and rubbed his arm.

"I'm so sorry. I didn't mean to do that." Her cheeks pinked.

"Don't worry. My sisters have done worse." They climbed up on the walkway over the dunes.

"How many?"

"Three."

"Three?"

"And two brothers."

"Wow." She dragged her hand over the railing, skimming the dune grass.

"That must sound crazy to an only child."

"Crazy, no. Chaotic, maybe." She grinned at him.

"Most of the time, yes." He winked. "But I wouldn't have it any other way."

"This is my street. I guess I'll see you later." She turned to go.

He caught up with her. "Can I see you again?"

"Maybe. I'll see you at the store. No promises." She walked backward a few steps before turning and jogging away.

No promises.

He'd just have to make it happen, then.

Chapter Eleven

FRIDAY NIGHT HOPE RAN TO the door when the doorbell rang. She opened it to Ian standing there holding a picnic basket with a huge red bow on it.

"Isn't it a little late in the year for a picnic?"

"Not a picnic. Brought you a present."

Why would he bring her a present? It wasn't her birthday. No holiday she could think of. He stood there with that silly grin on his face. "Can I come in?"

Oh, gosh, how long had she kept him standing on the porch? "I'm sorry! Please!" She stepped back to let him in.

It took him just a few long strides to reach her couch. "Come, sit down." He patted the couch next to him.

She sat on the cushion beside him as he placed the basket on the floor at their feet.

"Sit back, and pull your feet up."

She gave him a quizzical look.

"Just trust me. And close your eyes."

She pulled her legs onto the couch and allowed her eyelids to slide shut. Ian's solid thighs bumped against hers as he reached into the basket, and then something soft and warm was placed into her lap.

Her eyes jerked open as the tiny fur ball moved. Big, green eyes peered out from a round, fuzzy head. A long tail swished against her legs. A barely audible mew squeaked past a pink tongue.

"Oh, Ian!" She gathered the kitten in her arms and lifted it for closer inspection and a kiss. "He's beautiful." She held him close and looked at Ian. "Why?"

"I wanted to see you smile." He leaned closer to pet the animal, and his musky scent surrounded her. "What are you going to name him?"

She swallowed hard as his shoulders rested against hers when he sat back. The warmth of his body spread throughout hers. "I- I'm not sure yet. I'll have to think about it."

He twisted in his seat toward her. "Did you eat yet? We could get a pizza, watch a movie."

"Sounds great." She unfolded one leg, but he put his hand on it. "I'll order it. Stay with your cat."

"He's a kitten."

"Fine. Kitten." He stood and walked a few paces away and pulled out his cell phone.

She watched his broad shoulders move under his yellow polo shirt as he raked his hand through his wavy, sun-bleached hair. She jerked back to attention when he snapped his phone shut.

"Twenty minutes. There's a great place about a mile from here."

"Of course there is."

He shrugged. "I grew up here. I know where everything is." He wandered to the kitchen and returned with plates, napkins and glasses, which he set on the coffee table. "I know you're not a native. So, when did you move to Maryland?"

"We moved here about six years ago. Then—"

"Here? To Brandon Beach?"

"Yeah. I moved here for my last semester of high school. Nice, huh?"

"Ouch."

"I finished high school and did my first two years of college at the tri-county community college, and then I went to Chicago, where we lived before Maryland, for the last two years of college."

"And you majored in English?"

"English Ed. I wanted to be a teacher."

His brows furrowed. "So why aren't you teaching?"

She sighed. "I followed my college boyfriend, Marcos, to Maryland. He told me there were plenty of teaching jobs in Montgomery County, but he was *so* wrong. Well, there were plenty of jobs for Spanish teachers, especially native speakers like him, but not English teachers like me. I took the tech writing job just to have something to live on. Maybe next year."

"And are you still with this boyfriend?"

"No. He turned out to be about as reliable as his information."

"Wow. I'm sorry."

She shrugged. "Not your fault."

"I guess that's why I never met you. I was at U Maryland the whole time you were here. I got my bachelor's there and then my MBA. I was here for the summers, but I don't remember you. I was almost always working, though."

"Trust me, we never shopped at your store." She winced. "No offense."

"None taken. Locals usually don't." He chuckled. "Should I get a movie?" He moved to the bookshelf near her TV. "Anything in particular?"

"I like all of them, so whatever you like."

He frowned as his fingers skimmed along the titles. "Are they all chick flicks?"

Just Until Christmas

"No, not all, tough guy." She stuck her tongue out.

He laughed, then selected a movie and grabbed the remote before sitting next to Hope again. He put his arm behind her on the back of the couch and his feet up on the table.

Hope raised her eyebrows at him. "Comfortable?"

"Very. Thanks." He flashed his dimples.

She leaned her head back on his arm.

"I like spending time with you." He tucked an errant strand of hair behind her ear.

The cat mewed and crawled across her lap into his.

"Hey, I brought some kitten food and two bowls. And a litter box, and litter."

"You're kidding."

"Nope. Everything you need. At least that's what the pet store said." He picked up the cat and headed into the kitchen.

Hope stood and watched, speechless, as Ian set the bowls on the floor, filled one with water and one with food, and then set up the litter box.

He came back to her side. "I have one more gift."

"Another one?"

He reached once more into the picnic basket, then handed her a red spray bottle and cat brush.

Hope's jaw dropped and her mouth went dry. "The blueberry wash? You remembered?"

"I remember a lot."

She threw her arms around his neck. "Thank you."

"Well that was a surprise." His voice was low in her ear.

She drew back, keeping her arms looped around his neck. "Impulse. Sorry."

"I'm not." His sapphire eyes searched her soul as his hands slowly settled at her waist.

Her breath hitched. She withdrew her hands, played wither necklace.

"Ian ... I'm only here until Christmas."

His smile faded. "Only until Christmas? Then you're leaving?"

Was that disappointment in his eyes? Didn't matter. She wasn't staying. Her decision, not his. Not this time.

She stepped away—away from his scent, away from his warmth, away from any power he might begin to have over her.

"Yes. I have to go back to Bethesda."

He gave her a crooked smile. "Oh."

The doorbell chimed. *Thank goodness.*

"Pizza's here." He opened the door to retrieve dinner then set it on the coffee table.

They chattered about safer topics as they polished off the pizza, and the tension faded. Hope finished her last slice and picked up the cat. "I'm going to name him Muffin."

"Muffin?" Ian laughed. She felt his chest rumble beside her as she settled back on the couch, Muffin curled up on the couch next to her.

Ian put his arm behind her again, so she slid closer to him. Not quite touching him, but enough to enjoy his presence.

He pressed "play" on the remote.

She sighed and focused on the Sandra Bullock film she'd seen a dozen times, trying to ignore the gorgeous man next to her. All she had to do was remember that no matter how nice he seemed now, he would eventually end up just like all the others.

Chapter Twelve

HE KNOCKED ON HER DOOR at precisely 7 pm. The late fall breeze blew through the porch and the calla lilies on the railing danced gently. The scent of the ocean and the squawks of seagulls wafted in from the beach.

No answer. He waited a few moments, then knocked again.

She answered almost immediately. "Did you knock before? I was upstairs. I couldn't tell if I heard a knock or not." She gestured for him to come inside. "Just let me get my shoes on."

As she pulled on white tennis shoes, he took in her long legs clad in faded jeans, the blue blouse that hugged her waist, and the pearl pendant that hung around her neck. Her blond hair was for once hanging freely down her back instead of pulled up. He hadn't realized how long it was.

"Where are we eating?" She tilted her head and smiled. She was wearing lipstick. Not a lot. Just a hint of soft pink.

"What are you hungry for?"

"Oh, just about anything. Mexican. Chinese. Not fond of Italian, though."

"There's a great Chinese restaurant not too far from here. One of my favorites. Sound good?"

"Sounds great." She grabbed her purse and headed for the front door.

He reached the door first and opened it for her. Her familiar citrus scent filled the air as she passed him.

The restaurant was on the small side, a typical Chinese establishment. It sported lots of red on the walls, round tables, a fish tank against the wall near the entrance.

Ian led Hope to a table in the corner. A young, strawberry-blond man fairly bounced up to the table. "Hi, my name is Josh. I'll be taking care of you tonight. May I get you a drink to start?" He spoke rapidly, barely taking a breath.

"Um, yeah, I'll take a Coke. Hope?"

"The same."

"You got it." Josh sped off.

Hope laughed. "At least he's perky."

"He's new. I've never seen him here before. Usually it's just family working. But I do remember the daughter left for college, now that I think about it."

"I think he could replace two people."

Ian chuckled. "You're probably right.

Hope's cell phone rang just as Josh finished taking their order. She winced and let it go to voicemail.

"Everything OK?"

"Don't worry about it." She shrugged and smiled, but her eyes went dark.

"I do worry about it. I worry about you."

"I don't need you worrying about me." She rearranged the silverware beside her plate, moving the spoon from one side of the knife to the other and back again.

He placed his hand on hers. "Hope, that's the fourth time I've seen you react that way to a phone call. Something is very wrong, and I'd like to help if you'll let me."

Her brow furrowed. "Four times?"

"That I've seen. Which means there are probably many more."

She let out a breath of frustration. "I owe a lawyer a lot of money back in Chicago. They keep calling about it."

"They won't let you make payments or anything?"

"I was, every month, but now they want it all."

He leaned on his forearms. "Will you let me help you? I have some money saved up. You can get them off your back, and pay me back whenever you can. I won't hassle you like they do." He grinned at her, but she only speared him with a harsh stare.

"I don't need to be rescued, Ian MacKay. You think I can't take care of myself? That I'm incapable just because I'm a woman?" She narrowed her eyes, now the color of spinach. "Or is it that I'm obviously too stupid to keep myself out of legal trouble and therefore need to be looked after?"

Ian put up his hands in surrender. "None of that!" He glanced at the patrons whose attention they had drawn and leaned in again. "I just see your face every time you get one of those calls. And I would do anything to keep you from pain."

The anger melted from her face. "I'm sorry. I shouldn't have taken it out on you like that." She rested her face in her hands for a few moments, then ran her fingers through her hair. "It's certainly not your fault."

He took her hand in both of his. He wanted to kiss it, but thought better of it.

"The debt is not my fault. It's my father's. But I still have to pay the legal fees. My lawyer was great. I loved her, but she moved to California, and the bill went to the collections department, and they haven't been nearly as understanding."

"Hope, please let me help you." He'd get down on his knees and beg if it would keep him from seeing that fear in her eyes again when the phone chimed.

"Ian, I barely know you. I can't take your money." She shook her head.

"We'll draw up a note. You can sign something if it makes you feel better."

"I don't know …"

"Will you at least think about it?"

"All right, guys. Here we go." Josh slid glasses of Coke and empty teacups out of the way. We've got spring rolls. General Tso's chicken. Careful. Plate's hot. And sesame beef. White rice. May I bring you anything else?"

"No, thanks, Josh. I think that will do for now." Ian nodded.

"Okay, then. Back later." He wheeled around and headed for another table.

"So, will you?" Ian scooped out some chicken onto his plate, and offered some to Hope. She held out her plate, and he served her as well.

"Will I what?" She grabbed the rice.

He sighed. "Think about it."

"Yeah, I'll think about it. If only to get you off my back. I don't need you on me as well as the lawyers." She made a goofy face at him.

"Hey, whatever it takes." He chuckled.

"Whatever what takes?"

"Whatever it takes to keep those green eyes sparkling."

Chapter Thirteen

HE WALKED HER TO THE door at the end of the evening. "Why don't you come to church with me tomorrow morning?"

"I don't think so."

"Why not? You said you believe in God?"

"Of course."

"Are you a Christian?"

"I am." She reached into her purse for the keys.

"Then what are you doing about worship? What have you been doing for the last month?"

"I read my Bible. I listen to preachers on TV on Sunday morning."

"Hope, you know that's not the same thing."

"It's the best I can do right now."

"The Bible reminds us we need each other, we shouldn't neglect coming together to worship."

"I know, but ..." She leaned against the door.

"But what?"

"I can't afford to get too connected here. It's bad enough …"

"Bad enough what?"

"Nothing."

"Bad enough you've allowed yourself to make one friend already?"

"I didn't mean it."

"Yeah, you did." He stared at the porch floor. "You can't cut yourself off from everyone for three whole months."

"I can try."

"Hope …"

"Hey, look, it's late. How about we finish up some other time?"

At 10:15 Sunday morning Hope's phone rang. Who would call so early on a Sunday morning?

"Hope? It's Ian."

Panic gripped her. "Ian? What's wrong?"

"Nothing. I'm picking you up in half an hour for church."

Uggh. "Ian, we talked about this."

"You talked."

"And apparently you didn't listen." Would it be too rude to just hang up?

"And neither did you. This is not good for you. Get dressed. It's a beach church. Jeans are fine."

"Ian…"

"Hope." He dragged out her name. "I'll be there in thirty minutes. And if you don't answer the door, I'll sit on your porch all day long. You know I will."

"Fine." She slammed her finger onto the end button.

Half an hour later his black jeep pulled up in front of her house. She came out so he wouldn't have to park.

She couldn't think of anything to say on the ten-minute drive to the south edge of town. She closed her eyes and gathered her courage as he walked around the car to open her door.

He held out his hand. "Come on, it will be fine. No one will attack you and demand a deep and abiding friendship today. I promise."

His smile disarmed her, and she relaxed in spite of herself. He put his hand on the small of her back to guide her and warmth spread from his touch to her shoulders, her neck. She shifted her purse to the shoulder nearest him as some sort of flimsy, cloth buffer.

Inside, he sat about a fourth of the way up, on the aisle. Various members smiled, but since the service was just about to start, no one spoke to them. She glanced around the small church, its white walls, deep cherry wood-colored pews, blue carpet. The dais was raised about two feet, making it easy to see the pulpit from even the back rows.

The worship leader came to the front with a guitar and invited everyone to stand. He began singing a familiar chorus, three singers to his left joining him.

Hope startled at Ian's strong, tenor voice. Most of the guys she knew back in her church in Bethesda barely sang aloud. They never prayed aloud like Ian had so often before meals. His faith was so different, so much a part of him.

After another song or two, the pastor spoke about hope. She laughed silently at the irony. Her own name and yet she felt she had none.

Pastor Fitzgerald said they should "be strong and take heart, all you who hope in the LORD." Well how was she supposed to do that, exactly? Just will herself to be strong, take heart? She'd been trying.

He directed them to Psalm 25:5. "Guide me in your truth and teach me, for you are God my Savior, and my hope is in you all day long." For God to guide us in His truth, the pastor said, we need to listen to His truths, listen to his voice.

Had Hope been listening? She'd told Ian she'd been reading her Bible, but that wasn't really true. She glanced at it now and then, but she wasn't paying attention to what God had to say to her. Not really.

Next to her, Ian put his arm on the pew behind her. He never touched her, but she felt ... protected, enclosed. Surrounded by his faith. On his lap sat his Bible and a note pad. He was taking notes? She'd never seen anyone her age takes notes on a sermon before. Only the old ladies at home took notes, and she was never sure what they did with them.

She drew her attention back to Pastor Fitzgerald. He read from Psalms 33. Hope found the chapter in her own Bible.

"But the eyes of the LORD are on those who fear Him, on those whose hope is in his unfailing love, to deliver them from death and keep them alive in famine. We wait in hope for the LORD; He is our help and our shield. In Him our hearts rejoice, for we trust in His holy name. May Your unfailing love be with us, LORD, even as we put our hope in You."

So that was the idea. Put your hope in His unfailing love. Trust in His name. She wasn't sure how to do that.

As the worship leader returned to the dais and the congregation stood, Ian brought his face near her ear. He smelled of musk and salt air and she took a deep breath to keep from burying her face in his neck.

He gently grasped her elbow as he whispered, "Let's go."

She followed him out of the pew and the building. "Why are we leaving early? The service isn't over yet."

"This way you won't have to talk to anyone." He flashed one of his by-now familiar dimpled grins at her as they crossed the parking lot.

He'd do that for her? Give up part of his church time for her?

As he held her door to the Jeep open, he ran his hand down her arm. "How about lunch? I know a great place a few miles further in. Quiet, no beach crowd, no one from church. OK?"

All she could manage was "OK."

Ian spent the drive in telling her about the church, its local history, the pastor, and some of its more colorful members.

She spent the time letting his calm voice soothe her frayed nerves, and watching his muscled arms maneuver the Jeep through the potted back roads.

"So did you like the church, or am I in trouble for kidnapping you?"

That smile. How could he stay in trouble for any length of time when his smile made her stomach do somersaults like that? "No, I really liked it. It's quite different from my church in Bethesda."

"How so?"

"For one thing, the pastor's sermon was actually useful."

Ian chuckled. "Your pastor's sermons aren't useful?"

"Not really. Not like that one. He'll go through some Bible story or passage, but he never really tells us how to use it in our lives like your pastor did today."

"OK. How else is it different?"

"Well, you're different from any of the guys in my church."

"Uh-oh."

"No, that's a good thing."

"Then how am I different?"

"Well, none of them would ever sing out loud like you did. And no one my age would *ever* take notes."

Ian laughed. "Really?"

"No way. What do you do with them, anyway?"

"Sometimes nothing. Just writing it down helps cement it in my brain. Sometimes I look back at it over the week as I study the Bible on my own."

He studied the Bible on his own? "Are you in seminary or something?"

Another laugh. "No. Why?"

Fortunately they pulled into the parking lot before she had to explain a question that was obviously funnier than she had intended.

Chapter Fourteen

AS THE TIME CREPT PAST noon, the sun poured in a side window of the restaurant and played with the highlights in her hair. Ian loved her hair, loved when she wore it down instead of yanked back in a ponytail. The women in his family were all brunettes, and Katie was a brunette …

Blonde was different. So many different colors of blond on one head. Fascinating. And those green eyes. When she talked about something she cared about, they lit up. When she was hiding, they grew dark, as if a door closed shut on them. Then he couldn't see into them no matter how hard he tried.

Ian watched her as she finished her Coke. He'd had enough small talk. He wanted—needed—to know why she was only going to be here until Christmas. Until now, she hadn't seemed willing to talk about it. But they'd been spending more and more time together, almost every Friday, and at least a couple other days a week, so maybe now she'd open up.

Just Until Christmas

"So, Hope, you want to tell me why you are here only until Christmas?"

She sighed, and ran her teeth over her bottom lip. A nervous habit, he'd learned.

She pushed her plate away and leaned on her arms.

He checked her eyes. No closed door yet.

"Short answer? My father conned someone into a bad deal. Back in Chicago, where we lived before here. He died. They sued for the beach house. He put it in both our names as soon as I was twenty-one. I won, but I still had to pay the lawyers and court costs. I can sell the house, but I have to live in it three more months to meet the residency requirement to avoid huge capital gains taxes. The time will be up December 21. Then I'm going back to Bethesda."

Ian's heart sank. That explained everything. Her obsessive need to fix the house, her unwillingness to connect with anyone, the three-month mystery. "No other options?"

"None that I can think of. I just need to sell it and get back home."

Home. He swallowed past the lump in his throat. "Is there someone in Bethesda you need to go back to?"

She looked at him, almost right through him. "No. There's just nothing here."

He'd change that if she'd let him.

He settled into his seat in the Jeep. The day couldn't be over yet. "How about a walk through the Farmer's Market?"

"Oh, that would be great. I'd love some fresh fruit."

"You got it." He pointed the vehicle toward the road. Once there, he followed her down the rows, carrying a wicker basket while she selected peaches, corn, even a watermelon. After paying for the food, over her objections, they went for a long drive through the farmland of the Eastern Shore before returning home.

Ian carried the paper bag of produce in and set it on her counter.

"How about a milkshake? I need to give you something for all your effort."

He turned around and leaned back against the Formica. "Yeah, it was a lot of hard work to carry all that food around."

"Gotta give those muscles a workout somehow." She placed her hands on his biceps. He could swear her breath hitched.

His definitely did. The heat remained when she removed her hands.

"Could you get a couple glasses down? The tall ones?" She pointed to the cupboard behind him.

"Sure," he said. But he didn't move for several moments, instead watching her every move as she took out ice cream and milk from the appliance across from him.

She set the items down and turned to him. "Well?" Her eyebrows rose.

"Sorry." He turned and reached behind him. Did guys blush? He hoped not. He handed her the glasses and tried to decide if she were smirking.

As the clock neared 6 pm, he hovered near the door, unwilling to end the day, unwilling to end any day that would bring him closer to her leaving.

"I had a great time today, Hope." He ran the tips of his fingers down her cheek, and was rewarded with a smile before she dropped her head.

He hooked his finger under her chin and gently pulled her face up toward his. Moving his hand to her cheek, he placed his other hand on her waist as he brought his lips to hers.

Her mouth was warm and soft, and when she responded to his kiss, his pulse kicked into overdrive. He slid his hand around her back and drew her closer.

Although he could have kissed her all night, he pulled back, stared into the emerald abyss of her eyes.

"Ian …" Her voice was uncertain.

His feelings weren't. But he couldn't have her scared. He leaned his forehead against hers. "It's just a goodnight kiss, Hope," he whispered. "It's OK."

She seemed to relax, so he kissed her cheek before he slipped out her door.

Sitting in his Jeep, though, he knew it wasn't OK. He was falling, fast.

And he only had a short while to win her heart.

Just until Christmas.

Chapter Fifteen

HOPE TURNED UP THE MUSIC from her iPhone as she ran that night, trying to block her thoughts. She'd thought about running on the beach, but it only made her think of him. Instead, she opted for the route she'd taken when she first arrived—down Ocean View to New York Avenue, then south for half an hour. Turn around and come home. Kind of boring, but effective.

She ran hard the last few minutes of her run, but no matter what she did she couldn't erase the memory of Ian's kiss.

This was not good. She couldn't get involved with him. She'd told him she was leaving before Christmas. What could have possessed him to do that? What possessed her to let him?

As she neared the corner she slowed. Chest heaving, she turned down the music and reviewed her priorities.

First, she needed to get the house fixed up. Second, she must make as much money as possible in the meantime to pay off the lawyer's fees. Third, she had to get the house on the market so she could sign the

Just Until Christmas

papers on December 21st.

Her breathing calmed and her heartbeat slowed to its regular rhythm. She turned onto Ocean View Parkway.

Once all that was accomplished, she had to get out of Brandon Beach and away from Ian. That was the only way she could be safe.

To be fair, it wasn't like she'd asked Ian to stop. So far he'd proven to be different from most other guys she'd known. He was generous, kind, gentle. He didn't give unwanted advice. He listened when she talked. And yesterday was by far the most enjoyable day she'd had in ... well, years.

Maybe that pastor was right. What was it he said? *Put your hope in His unfailing love.* Did she have any hope in God? She was always hedging her bets. Always had a backup plan. Never took any risks, played it safe.

Maybe because Dad had done nothing but take risks. He'd dragged her from city to city to city, never putting down roots. Never teaching her how to do the same. The longest they'd stayed anywhere was Chicago, so at least she could get a recommendation from a former high school teacher to get into the university there for her last two years of study.

Since then every time she had taken a risk, she'd lost. Moved to Maryland with Marcos? She was left tin a new state without a job. Trusted Steve with the handling the preparations for the presentation to the university? Cut out of it entirely. And lost out on the promotion. Believed Chris every time he said he was at a sales meeting? Yeah, right.

But had she sought the Lord about any of those decisions? Put her hope in Him? Or just barreled ahead on her own and expected Him to follow?

Put your hope in Him.

But how? She had enough trouble trusting people she could see, hear, touch. How was she supposed to trust *God?*

That was something she'd never gotten a handle on.

Perhaps it was time to learn.

Chapter Sixteen

IAN LAY IN BED MONDAY morning, exhausted after little sleep. The last time he'd looked at the clock the red numbers blinked 3:17 at him, over and over. He'd been awake for at least an hour after that. Every time he closed his eyes he heard her uncertain voice saying his name. But he also felt her lips on his, and those two sensations collided in his mind, making sleep impossible.

He replayed the kiss over and over. Her hands had been on his chest, not around his neck or waist, but she hadn't pushed him away, either. And she hadn't scolded him for it. How much trouble was he in with her?

"Dude!"

Ian looked up to see Rob standing in the doorway to the office, arms akimbo. When did he come in? "What?" His voice came out harsher than intended.

"What's with the attitude? What did *I* do?"

Just Until Christmas

"Nothing. Sorry."

Rob took the chair next to the desk and started tossing the nerf ball. "It's her, isn't it? What now?"

"I kissed her."

"Wouldn't that be a good thing?"

Ian groaned. "She's only here until Christmas."

"So then why did you kiss her?"

Ian jumped up, throwing his hands in the air. "I don't know. We spent all day together yesterday. I picked her up for church. We went to lunch, to the farmer's market, back to her house. I had to force myself to leave. But first I kissed her goodnight."

The nerf ball stilled. "A kiss, or a *kiss*?"

Ian had nothing to say.

"Oh." For once Rob didn't laugh at him.

"I tried to pass it off as nothing, but I have never felt this way, not even with Katie."

"You can't make her stay if she doesn't want to, dude. You know that."

"I know." Ian paced for a moment. "So do I apologize, ignore it, what?"

"I think if you bring it up, you may draw too much attention to it. Try just pretending it never happened. If she brings it up, then talk about it. Follow her lead."

Pretend it never happened. Right.

Ian walked to the tinted window that overlooked the store. "Think it would be all right to ask her to my house for Thanksgiving? I mean, she doesn't have anyone else. I just don't want her to be alone that day."

"You can ask. Don't push."

"I won't push."

"That's what you said about Katherine."

He spun around. "And I learned my lesson, didn't I? The hard way!" He exhaled a long breath. "Sorry, didn't mean to yell again."

"I don't know. *Did* you learn?"

"I did. I'm not going to kiss her. I'm not going to ask her to stay. I just want to be her friend. Seriously."

"That's *all* you want?"

"OK, I admit, I would like more. But I'm not *asking* for more."

He threw the ball again. "All right. Keep that in mind."

Friday night after they finished their pizza and a movie, Ian set the remote on the coffee table and twisted to face her. "Would you like to come to my parents' house for Thanksgiving? I mean, if you don't already have plans? It's casual, just my family. My brothers and sisters and their families. And Rob."

"I don't know…" She stroked Muffin's head as he meowed in her lap.

"What else are you going to do? Sit home and eat a turkey sandwich?"

She squared her shoulders. "Maybe. What's so bad about that?"

"Nothing. Look, no pressure. You don't have to come. I'm just offering. I thought you might want to be around some other people that day."

She drew her teeth over her bottom lip.

He'd better ease off. "Hey, one more or less isn't going to make a difference in the amount of food my mom and sisters make, so you don't have to decide right now. It's not until next week. I'll ask you next Wednesday, OK?"

"Sounds good."

He scratched the kitten's head. "Muffin has to stay home, though."

"No fair." She pouted.

"Ok, fine. If it'll make you come, bring him."

She giggled. "I don't think that'll help."

He picked up the kitten and held him up. "Will you talk to her? Convince her to come?"

The animal mewed.

"You will? Good. I need her there."

She gently took Muffin back. "And why is that?"

"'Cause you're what I'm most thankful for this year."

Chapter Seventeen

HOPE CLOSED HER EYES AGAINST the noise. Women chattered. Little boys chased each other. Girls giggled. Pots and pans clanged.

She took air in through her nose and blew it out through her mouth, like she'd seen pregnant women on television do. To say the walls were closing in might be a little extreme, but it was becoming more and more difficult to breathe. It felt like there was a metal band around her chest, slowly tightening with each person that came and talked to her. Hugged her. Bubbled and smiled and gushed over the joy of life. There were just way too many people in this house.

And dinner hadn't even started yet. They probably went around and said what they were thankful for. While holding hands.

She had to find Ian. Why had he abandoned her? She skirted around his sisters decorating the tree, avoided the nephews playing with the toy cars, and found him leaving the kitchen. "I have to go."

His jaw hung open a moment. "Why?" He set the basket of warm rolls on the table.

"I just do." She hurried to the front closet and hunted for her jacket, shoving sweaters and coats aside.

"Then I'll go with you."

"Don't." She put her hand on his chest, held him at arm's length. "Just stay."

"Hope ... talk to me." He tried to catch her eyes.

She avoided his gaze. She couldn't let his warmth suck her back in. "Can't."

"But why? Why are you leaving?" He reached for her arm.

"I just can't deal with all ... this." She shrugged him off and opened the front door.

"OK. Then we'll leave together." He followed her onto the front porch, closing the door behind him.

She scoffed. "You'd leave your family. Why would you do that?"

"Because I care about you."

"You're not my boyfriend."

"I'm your friend."

"Only for three more weeks."

"Why? Why does it have to end then?"

Shrugging on her jacket, she hurried down the driveway. "Just go inside, Ian. Go to your family, and leave me alone."

"I don't want to leave you alone."

She halted and turned to face him. "I've always been alone. And the last couple months have been a nice diversion, but they really didn't change anything."

"Hope, you have explain this to me. Help me understand what's going on here."

Rubbing her forehead, she sighed deeply. "My mom died when I was twelve, right?"

"Yes." He tried to take her hand, but she pulled it away.

"I lived with my father, but he couldn't really deal with it. We moved around a lot. I went to a different school every year, sometimes two. I never really knew my extended family—aunts, uncles, cousins. It was just me and my dad, and he wasn't really there, you know? I'm just not used to all this ... togetherness. There are just too many people in there for me, and they all want to talk to me and get to know me and be nice to me and they're all so happy ... " It was just so ... not her.

He placed his hands on her shoulders, and drew them gently down her arms until he reached her hands. OK. I can understand that." His voice was soft. "Then let me take you somewhere else. My house. Your house. We'll go someplace quiet, just the two of us. Please don't go home all alone. It's not good for you."

She crossed her arms over her chest. "Says who? You're not my boyfriend, and you're not my father. You don't get to tell me what to do." She kept her tone gentle, but he wasn't going to control her.

"I'm not trying to. I'm begging you to let me help you. If you won't, I'll turn around and go back inside. But I'd rather be with you. We can take some food home from here, or get a pizza. Then we can go to your house, or mine, and watch a movie, or do whatever you want. Your call entirely."

Was he serious? Could she trust him? She wanted to. "OK. My house. You bring the food. Turkey, Chinese, whatever you want. I'll wait for you."

His eyes lit up like the lights on the tree in his living room. "I'll grab my jacket and be there in half an hour." He cupped her face and placed a kiss on her cheek before bounding back up the drive.

Those blue eyes were so hard to resist. Hopefully, they hadn't just sweet-talked her into a huge mistake.

Chapter Eighteen

IAN PUNCHED THE SPEED DIAL on his phone and heard it ring twice.

"Ian?"

"Feel like going shopping?"

She laughed. "The day after Thanksgiving? Are you insane?"

"I didn't know how hardcore a shopper you were."

"Not that hard. Besides, I think stores should all be closed today. Let the workers stay home with their families. I think Black Friday is a terrible idea. Wait ... are you open today? I didn't just insult you, did I?"

He chuckled. "No, we're closed. Want to do something? Or do you have to work, or do stuff for the house?" *Please say no.*

"Nope, I'm not working today, and I only have a celling fan left for the house, and it's on backorder."

"Let me know when it comes in and I'll put it in for you."

"Thanks. That would be wonderful. Then I can get it listed and get it sold. What did you have in mind for today?"

"We could drive down to see the ponies. Or we could probably find a tree lighting somewhere."

"The ponies—oh, I always wanted to see them. Let's do that."

"OK. Be there in fifteen."

When he pulled up to her house, she was waiting on the porch. He hopped out of his jeep and walked around to her side of the car. "You look beautiful today."

"Thank you. You look good in red." She pointed to his sweater.

"Oh. My mom gave it to me. One of the last gifts she picked out." Pain pricked his heart for a moment.

"She did good." She patted his chest.

"She was always good at picking out clothes for people." He closed her door and climbed in his seat.

About an hour into the ride, her phone rang. She glanced at the number and silenced it. Fifteen minutes later, it rang again.

"Aren't you going to answer that?"

"No." She stared out the window.

"Chicago again?"

She huffed and turned to him. "What makes you say that?"

"'Cause only Chicago gets you worked up like that. They call on the day after Thanksgiving?"

"My time is up on Monday. They're getting very antsy."

"Do you have the money?"

She was silent.

He pulled the jeep to the side of the road and jerked up the emergency brake. "What happens if you can't pay?"

"I don't know." Her voice cracked. "It's so not fair. It's not my fault my father was a crook."

"Hope, please let me help you." He rubbed her back.

She studied her hands. "I hate feeling so helpless."

"Borrowing money to get out of a situation you fell into through no fault of your own does not mean you're helpless. Or dumb, or anything else you're thinking I might be thinking. I believe you are a strong, brave, resourceful, and beautiful woman who needs to learn to accept help."

"What about you?"

"Me what?"

"Do you ever accept help?"

"Rob just invested in the store. In this economy, it might not have survived otherwise. Now he owns nearly half of what has been a MacKay store for generations, and has made some significant changes. That also allowed my father to retire earlier than he planned to stay home and care for my mom."

"Wow. I never would have guessed."

"Why?"

She shrugged. "You just seem to have … everything … all together all the time."

"Like I keep trying to tell you, it's not a weakness to let others in." How had she developed armor so unbelievably tough?

Her phone trilled.

"Now, not that I'm telling you what to do,"—he grinned—"but I think you should answer that. Tell them you'll have all the money first thing Monday morning. When we get back we can draw up an agreement if you want. We can even see my lawyer if it makes you more comfortable. And we'll transfer the money to your account as soon as the banks open."

The phone chimed again. She answered it, and delivered the message.

"Better?" He tucked a loose strand of hair behind her ear and left his hand on her cheek.

"Yeah, actually. Thanks."

"Any time. How about some ponies?"

She placed her hand over his. "Ponies it is."

He released the parking brake and steered the jeep back onto the road.

Why did she have to be going back so soon? And why was his heart betraying him? He kept telling himself he had no business falling in love, but there seemed to be no way to stop it.

Chapter Nineteen

HOPE WASN'T QUITE READY WHEN Ian knocked. She peeked thorough the sidelights. He looked great, as usual. Jeans, a black t-shirt, sport coat.

She pulled the door open. "Hey, I need just a few more minutes."

"Why? You look perfect." There was that smile.

"Let me grab a sweater. Movie theaters are always cold."

"I could keep you warm." He grinned.

I'm sure you could. "Just stop." She laughed as she opened the hall closet and chose a pink sweater to go with the white blouse she was wearing.

"Hey, I heard that the high school is looking for an English teacher for next semester."

She clenched her teeth. "I won't be here next semester."

"You didn't seem all that eager to go back to Bethesda last time we talked."

"Doesn't mean I'm looking for a job." She called from the kitchen as she locked the back door.

"I'm just passing on something I heard."

"You sure that's all it is?"

"What do you mean?"

"Sure you're not trying to find a way to keep me here?"

"Keep you here? Wha—"

She tried to slow her breathing. "Seems to me you've been doing a lot of things to try to make me want to stay here."

"Like what?"

"You keep telling me how beautiful it is here—"

"It *is* beautiful. I love it here. I grew up here. After I graduated I could have gone anywhere. I chose to come back here!"

She put her fists on her hips. "And there's the money."

"They were going to garnish your wages! What would you have done for food? I was only trying to help. How is that keeping you here? You can pay me back from anywhere, any time. We put that in writing, at your request."

"That's not all. There's the kitten."

He squeezed his eyes shut. "The kitten?"

"Yeah, the kitten. What am I supposed to do with him when I leave? Drag him on a three-hour car trip? He'd be throwing up by the Bay Bridge."

"I thought of that. But I wanted to make you happy while you were here. And if you decided you couldn't take him with you I would have no problem finding that kitten a home. Any little girl would love her."

"Are you calling me a little girl now?"

"Oh, my—No! Where did you get that? Are you crazy?" He threw his hands in the air.

"Apparently! I never should have trusted you. I thought you were a friend, someone I could have fun with while I was here."

"I am your friend. I care deeply about you. I'm just passing on information, trying to give you options. Believe me, I would never tell you what to do."

"Sure you would. It's what you've been doing all along." She stomped away.

"Hope, what are you talking about?"

"All these little things you've been doing. You've just been setting me up."

"Hope, I swear I'm not trying to control you. Forget about the job. Forget I ever said anything. Can we just go to the move and have a nice evening?"

"No! We can't just forget about it! I think you should leave."

"Leave?"

She crossed her arms. "Yes. You should leave."

He reached for her. "Hope, please talk to me. I really don't understand what happened here."

She backed away. "You need to go."

Ian swallowed hard. "Hope, I don't know what I did, but I am sorry. I would never hurt you. You have no idea how much I care about you." Shoulders slumped, he turned and left, closing the door behind him.

So it had finally happened. She should have known it wouldn't last.

Chapter Twenty

"SO BEFORE I KNOW IT, she's kicking me out of her house and I don't even know what I did wrong." Ian slammed the desk drawer shut, flinching at the sound reverberating through the office.

"What *exactly* did she say?" Rob gently closed the drawer that had bounced open.

"She said I was trying to control her. That loaning her the money, giving her the kitten, and telling her about this job were all ways to try to control her and make her stay here in Brandon Beach."

"And were you?"

"No! You know I know better than that. She said she hated her job, she wanted to teach, so I told her about the opening at the community college. That's *all*." He stood and paced in front of the desk. "But now, I'm like all the other men in her life, secretly out to micromanage her entire life as part of some huge, evil plot."

Rob leaned against the desk.

"I don't know what to do now."

"Do? You stay away, dude. At least for a while."

"Shouldn't I apologize?"

"Not now. She can't hear it. You've got to give her time to calm down. She's smart. Give her some space and let her think it out. She'll realize you aren't evil. Doesn't mean you'll have a chance with her, but I think she'll see you didn't mean anything by what you said."

"I hope so. I don't want her to hate me. I don't expect to have a chance with her, but I really do want to be her friend."

"If you really want what's best for her, stay away for now, and pray for her."

"I've been praying for her. Every day."

"Then do what you told her to do. Put your hope in Him. Wait on the Lord."

Chapter Twenty-one

A KNOCK ON THE DOOR was followed by the sound of it slowly opening. Hope glanced up from her spot on the couch.

"Rob. What are you doing here?"

"Ian told me you'd bought a new ceiling fan and he was going to help you put it in. He didn't think he should come over now."

Hope set aside her book and unwrapped herself from the blanket. "He's right about that. I'm still very angry with him."

"So I've heard. But if you'll get me the fan, I'll put in in for you."

"Why?"

"So it will be ready for you to sell. Or stay. Or whatever. I don't know. He just asked me to help you."

"He did?" Why would Ian help her get the house ready to sell if he wanted her to stay? That didn't make sense. But still…

"Yes. Is this it on the table?" He moved to the dining room.

"Yeah. It is. I'll get a step ladder."

Just Until Christmas

"Thanks. May I move the coffee table?"

"Sure." She returned with the ladder and grabbed the other end of the table.

Rob climbed up and unscrewed the old fan from the ceiling.

"There's nothing I hate more than being lied to. He had this all planned from the start."

"Had what planned from the start?"

"He's been trying to keep me here. The kitten, the loan, the job. He made it all sound so innocent, but he's trying to control me. I won't stand for it."

"Hope, I really don't want to get between you two, but may I tell you a few things?"

She eyed him for several long seconds before agreeing.

He stepped back down. "First, Ian wasn't trying to arrange anything. He grew up here. He knows people and he hears things and he knows how to get things done. What you didn't give him a chance to tell you is that job is only for the next semester. The teacher is going on maternity leave and is returning in September. So if he were trying to keep you here with that, he wouldn't be doing a very good job."

Her cheeks heated. "Oh. I guess I didn't let him finish."

"Second, Ian learned the hard way that you can't make anyone stay with you who doesn't want to stay. It almost always backfires."

"What do you mean 'the hard way'?"

"He'd kill me if I told you. You're really leaving?"

"I don't see any other choice."

"In our last year of grad school, he fell in love with a girl named Katie. I never really liked her, but whatever. I didn't want to marry her."

"He was engaged?"

"Almost. She wanted to go see Europe, travel, live life, she said. He convinced her to stay with him, said they belonged together, he knew it, etc, etc. She did, for a while. She left about two months after graduation."

"Wow."

"So you see, he would never try to get you to stay here. No matter how badly he wanted you to. He really was just trying to help."

"But all that information ..."

"He was just passing on what he heard. He knew you would rather be teaching." He set down the screwdriver. "Hope, did you ever think maybe God had plans for you? Maybe it wasn't Ian's idea, but God's?"

"*I* made plans. Good plans. Financially sound plans. Why would God mess them up? Let others keep messing them up?"

"Proverbs 19 says 'Many are the plans in a person's heart, but it is the LORD's purpose that prevails.' Look, I'm not saying I know what God has in mind for your life. Maybe you are meant to go back to Bethesda. I'm just saying that maybe you should talk to God about it. I care about you, too, Hope. I consider you a friend, and I'd like to see you and Ian both happy, whether that's together or apart." He picked up the screwdriver and stepped back up on the ladder.

Hope slipped onto the porch.

She had a lot to think about.

Chapter Twenty-two

THREE WEEKS. IT HAD BEEN three weeks since Ian had talked to or even seen Hope. He had to let her go. He just didn't now how.

The bells over the door chimed. "I just ran into the realtor." Rob sauntered in. "She said she sold Hope's house last week. In three days. Hope priced it to sell. She'll be signing the papers and then leaving on the twenty-first, just like she wanted."

So it was done.

It wasn't so much that he'd lost the girl. He could live with that. It was that she thought so badly of him. He could deal with the fact that she didn't love him if she at least thought he was a decent person. Didn't put him in the same category with her father and her old boyfriend and that loser from work.

Was there any way he could change that?

What was it she'd said he'd done? The job offer, the money, the kitten… well, he couldn't take back telling her about the job, that was over and done with. The money ... if he hadn't loaned her the money, the law firm would have taken her car and her paycheck.

What about the kitten? He could offer to take the kitten for her. Find a home for him so she wouldn't worry about it. Maybe that would prove to her he'd hadn't meant to use the cat to keep her here.

That meant he had to go to her. Did she want to see him? Would she yell at him again?

She couldn't think any less of him, could she?

"What do you want, Ian? You better not be here to try and talk me out of leaving." She stood in the doorway, blocking his way.

"I just wanted to let you know that if it helps, I can take Muffin for you. I'll find him a good home, so you won't have to worry about him riding four hours in the car, or leaving him here in a shelter."

Her face softened. "Oh. You can?"

He pulled at the collar of his t-shirt. "Yeah. And if you need help with anything here after you leave, you can let me know, or Rob, if you'd rather."

"I think probably my real estate agent could handle anything I needed."

"Oh, OK. Thought I'd offer, just in case."

"Well, umm, thank you."

"So, do you want me to take Muffin now, or do you want to wait until the day you leave?"

"Well, I hate to give him up, but I close the day after tomorrow, so I guess it makes more sense if you take him now."

"OK." Why did his shirt feel so snug?

"Why don't you come on in and I'll get his stuff together?" She opened the door and stepped aside.

Her perfume surrounded him as he passed her. He hadn't realized how much he missed that.

"Have a seat."

He perched on the edge of her couch, and she picked up Muffin and plopped him in his lap. Ian held him up. "Hey, boy. You coming home with me today?"

Muffin gently pawed his face while she banged around in the kitchen.

"Yeah, I wish you could stay, too," he whispered.

Hope lugged out a flat-bottomed canvas bag full of Muffin's belongings. "Here's everything. I washed out the litter box and his food bowl, and there are some new toys. And here's a carrier to keep him safe in the car." She sat the blue and gray contraption on the coffee table. "He hates it, though."

"You've used it?"

"I had to take him to the vet. To get his shots."

His stomach soured. "Oh. I'm sorry. I didn't think. I didn't mean to cost you money."

"It's all right. He was worth it." She scooped him out of Ian's arms and buried her head in his fur. "I'm going to miss you." Her words were garbled, but he could make them out. She placed the cat on the flap of the carrier, coaxed him in and zipped it shut.

She stood up, her eyes misting. "Ian?"

"Yes?"

"Why are you doing this?"

"Doing what? Taking Muffin?"

She nodded.

"I'm just trying to help you get home."

"But I know you don't want me to go."

"Would I rather you stayed here? Maybe. I do care for you, Hope. And that means I want what's best for you, and I want you to be happy. You want to go back to Bethesda, so Muffin needs a new home."

"And what do you want from me in return?"

"In return?" Was she serious?

"Most people don't do something nice without wanting something."

"I just want you to be happy."

"That's all?"

"Well, one other thing."

She rolled her eyes. "I knew it."

"I want you to learn to trust God. Put your hope in Him."

Chapter Twenty-three

THE MILEPOSTS RACED BY HER on her way to the Bay Bridge. She'd forgotten how flat it was out here.

Her plants would be dead when she got home. She didn't get anyone to water them. Who would she ask? She didn't have any friends close enough who would come to her house for fifteen weeks in a row and water plants. Maybe if she'd been more active in church.

She should probably find a different one. Maybe one like Ian's. Was it at church he'd learned to do the things he did? Did his parents teach him to be so selfless? So caring?

She turned Ian's gesture over and over in her mind. He wasn't a cat person. He'd told her that. And he admitted her wanted her to stay in Brandon Beach. Yet he took Muffin to his house so she could leave.

And expected nothing in return.

Two days later, she sat in the pew, alone. She didn't know how to find a church like the one she'd attended in Brandon Beach with Ian, so she looked for one with a similar name. The music was familiar. She listened for a tenor voice like his, but there was none.

The sermon was about Hosea and Gomer. She tried to take notes, but she didn't know what to write.

Maybe she could write down the verses the pastor referenced, and look them up again later.

After church she ate her burger and fries on the couch watching a chick flick. She started to call for Muffin and then remembered she'd left him in Brandon Beach.

She sighed and put her feet on the coffee table. It wasn't the same without Muffin. She missed him curling up in her lap on lazy Sunday afternoons like this one, and chilly nights. Missed his meowing while she got ready in the morning. Missed him curled up at her feet while she wrote.

Who was she kidding?

She missed Ian. The Friday night movies and pizza. Mexican food in the middle of the week. Church on Sunday. His dimpled smile and blue eyes.

Was there a chance God had sent her to Brandon Beach? There were so many things that had lined up to cause her to end up there. The breakup with Chris. The fight with Steve. The residency requirement coming at just the right time. Then the job opening up there.

Coincidence? Or God?

But Ian said the job was only this semester. What then?

Put your trust in His unfailing love.

If this was God, surely He had something else planned.

She reached for her Bible. The notes with the Bible verses fell out. The pastor had taught from Hosea. Most of it had gone over her head. She never really read the Old Testament, but apparently the book was about Israel worshipping other gods. He'd started with chapter 10.

She skimmed the chapter listing the punishments God had in store for the unfaithful nation. Nothing she could use.

Just Until Christmas

Then that familiar phrase popped out at her.

Sow righteousness for yourselves, reap the fruit of unfailing love, and break up your unplowed ground; for it is time to seek the Lord, until he comes and showers His righteousness on you.

Was that a message just for her?

It is time to seek the Lord.

Did that mean she should go back to Brandon Beach? Trust Him to finish what He started?

Oh, God, please tell me what to do. If You want me to go back, please let me know somehow. I want to trust in You. I want to have hope. But I need You to show me how.

Chapter Twenty-four

FIVE MORE MILES. FIVE MORE miles and she would cross the city limits of Brandon Beach.

She'd prayed all day for four days. And every hour she felt more confident she belonged here. Would Ian still want her here? Would the job still be open? Where would she live? She had no answers to any of those questions.

She had never taken such a huge risk in her life.

She was putting her trust in His unfailing love.

Christmas Eve. Ian would probably be in church. She turned south, then left.

There were plenty of cars in the lot.

She parked in the last row and jogged, scanning every row for his Jeep. Not in this one, no … no … there—he must be here.

The last chorus of "Silent Night" was drawing to a close as she reached the door. She paced to the sounds of the pastor's benediction.

Just Until Christmas

Taking all three steps at once, she jumped off the landing and stood to the side. The double doors swung open. A few people wandered out, not in any hurry. Chatting, wishing Merry Christmas, hugging.

Come on ...

The crowd grew bigger and moved faster. Still no Ian. She chewed on her lower lip.

Wait...that was Logan, his brother. Wasn't it? And his sister, Isla. She could ask ... no, she'd just wait.

She returned to searching the exiting church-goers. The crowd was thinning. Still no Ian. What was he doing in there?

A tap on her shoulder startled her. She looked over her shoulder. "Rob?"

"Hope? I thought you were in Bethesda."

"I was. I came back."

"To stay? To visit? For Christmas?"

"To stay, I hope. Ummm, is Ian here? I saw the Jeep."

"Actually, he just left. He went out the side door."

Her heart sank. "Where did he go?"

"Home. To our apartment."

Now what? She'd never been to his place. They always watched movies at her house.

"I'm sure he'd be delighted to see you."

"Are you sure?"

He chuckled. "Oh, yeah. He's so in love with you." He grimaced. "Don't tell him I said that. Go to him. I was going to his parents' house, anyway."

"He's not going?"

"He was coming over in a bit. He's a little ... down. Go. The apartment is on Third. Second floor."

She got back in her Cruze. In five minutes she was outside his building taking deep breaths.

Three knocks—no one answered. Her heart sank. Maybe she'd been wrong all along.

Footfalls sounded inside. The doorknob turned, the door swung open.

"Hope. Wh -what are you doing here?"

"I came back."

"Why?"

Why? Wasn't he happy about it? "Well, I thought about what you said, and what Rob said, and I prayed about it, and I think it was God's plan that I come to Brandon Beach. So…I'm hoping that the job is still open."

"Come in. It's cold out." He closed the door behind her. Running his hand though his hair, he turned to face her. "You came back for the job?"

She shrugged off her coat and dropped it on a chair behind her. "If there are other things that are still available, I'll take those as well."

One corner of his mouth tipped up, revealing one dimple. "All of them?"

"Pizza nights, Mexican food …"

His blue eyes sparkled. "Help from a friend?"

She nodded, smiling up at him.

"Kisses?" He closed the distance between them.

She giggled. "Oh, yeah."

Hooking his fingers in the belt loops of her jeans, he pulled her against his chest. "I love you, Hope."

"I love you, too."

He lowered his head and covered her mouth with his, enfolding her in his arms.

He was warm and solid and real, and there wasn't a doubt in her mind this was where she belonged. He laid his forehead against hers. "So I take it you're not here just until Christmas?"

"Oh, yes, I am."

His head popped up, eyes wide. "What?"

"Christmas fifty years from now."

Laughter rumbled in his chest. "That, I can live with."

Also from Carole Towriss...

In the Shadow of Sinai

Journey to Canaan - Book 1

An artisan's world has been destroyed one too many times.

Can he conquer his anger to see his ability for what is—a gift from El Shaddai?

Or will he let his resentment rob him of his chance to build a masterpiece?

By the Waters of Kadesh

Journey to Canaan - Book 2

A young widow knows nothing but yesterdays filled th abuse and neglect. A displaced soldier anticipates nly empty tomorrows. A spy sees just a today he can manipulate to gain the power he craves.

Will they allow Yahweh to give them what they need?

The Walls of Arad

Journey to Canaan - Book 3

A young girl flees to save her life.
A vizier hides his faith from his king.
And a shepherd must become a warrior to save everything he holds dear.

I usually write Biblical fiction. I wrote most of *Just Until Christmas* when a publisher was looking for novellas for a Christmas anthology. It had to be set in a small town, and it had to be about Christmas. It was fun writing something when I didn't have to research nearly every single paragraph: Did they eat this fruit in this location? In this season? What fabric did they make their clothes from? What was the temperature in the summer?

The publisher closed its fiction division before they collected the stories, so it sat on a shelf. I decided to finish and release it.

I hope you enjoy it.

You can keep up with me and my new releases at www.caroletowriss.com.

Carole Towriss grew up in beautiful San Diego, California, and now lives just north of Washington, D. C. in a Maryland suburb. She shares her home with her husband of 30 years and their four children, Three of which are adopted from Kazakhstan. In between making tacos and telling her four children to pick up their shoes for the third time, she reads, watches chick flicks, writes and waits for summertime to return to the beach.

Made in the USA
Middletown, DE
01 June 2016